MICHAEL GARLAND
THE PRESIDENT and Mom's Apple Pie

Dutton Children's Books ★ *New York*

WILLIAM HOWARD TAFT (1857–1930) became the twenty-seventh president of the United States in March 1909. His real dream was to serve as a Supreme Court justice (a dream he fulfilled in 1920). In fact, he had no desire to run for president—it was his wife, Helen, who talked him into it. Taft never really enjoyed the job. Although he carried out his duties responsibly, it seemed to many Americans that what he liked best was watching baseball, playing golf, dancing, and spending time with his wife and their three children.

Taft was the first president to pitch a baseball at the opening of a major-league game, the first to have a presidential car, and the last to have a cow on the White House lawn to supply his family with fresh milk (the cow's name was Pauline). He loved to eat, and after a hearty meal would sometimes be caught napping during official functions. Nicknamed "Big Bill," Taft was our heaviest president, weighing in at over 300 pounds, but his portly stature never slowed him down much. He liked to travel and meet new people, and rode in trains all over the country to attend ceremonies dedicating big-city monuments as well as small-town flagpoles.

Copyright © 2002 by Michael Garland
All rights reserved.

CIP Data is available.

Published in the United States 2002 by
Dutton Children's Books,
a division of Penguin Putnam Books for Young Readers
345 Hudson Street, New York, New York 10014
www.penguinputnam.com

Designed by Daniel Hosek

Printed in Hong Kong
First Edition
ISBN 0-525-46887-0

1 3 5 7 9 10 8 6 4 2

For my niece Colleen

I remember that day in 1909 as if it were yesterday. President Taft was coming to our town to dedicate the new flagpole! No one had talked about anything else for weeks.

Main Street, decked out in red, white, and blue, was lined with people waiting for a glimpse of the President. I sat on my father's shoulders so I could see over all the heads. The Firemen's Band was playing "Hail to the Chief." I cheered with the crowd when the train finally whooshed into the station.

The train squealed to a halt, and I couldn't believe our luck. The doors slid open right in front of us. One man after another stepped down from the train. I didn't know any of them.

Finally another cheer rose from the crowd as William Howard Taft, the twenty-seventh president of the United States, filled the doorway. And I mean filled! He could barely squeeze through the door, but he was very nimble as he hopped down the steps.

As Mayor Jinks greeted the President, I slid down from my father's shoulders and jostled my way to the front. I could hear the mayor saying, "On behalf of the entire town, Mr. President, I welcome you. It is a tremendous honor to have you here. Come right this way."

The President stepped in the direction of the flag-pole, then suddenly stopped. He stood on tiptoe and sniffed the air.

"What is that wonderful aroma?" inquired the President. He had a dreamy look on his face.

Before anyone could answer, I called out, "Maybe it's Tony's Italian Villa! They make the best spaghetti in town."

"Lead the way, son!" the President said.

The crowd parted, and the President followed me down Main Street to Tony's, with the befuddled mayor, the Secret Service, the Firemen's Band, and the whole crowd trailing behind us.

Tony was very surprised to see the President approaching.

"How about some of that famous spaghetti I've heard so much about, Tony?" asked the President with a wink.

"Coming right up, Mr. President!" Tony said as he hurried toward the kitchen.

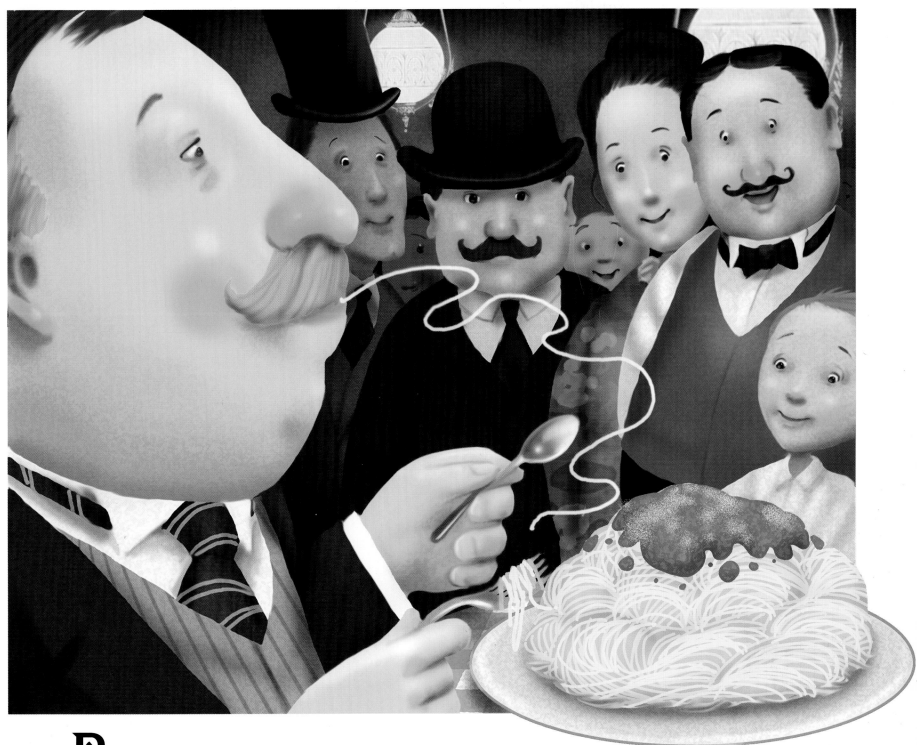

President Taft sat down and dug into a giant plate of spaghetti.

"That was excellent," he said when he had finished, "but it wasn't exactly what I was smelling."

"Could it be Big Ed's Barbecue across the street?" I suggested.

The President dashed across the street and ordered some of Big Ed's famous ribs. He nibbled and gnawed one after another. Then he wiped his face with a napkin and said, "Big Ed, those were the best ribs I've ever had, but they're not quite what I'm after."

"Mrs. Wong's Hunan Palace is on the corner," I said. "They have great food!"

At Mrs. Wong's, the President polished off a dish of steamed vegetables. "Delicious, but I'm on the trail of something different," he said as he marched outside.

"Mr. President! Let's not forget about the flagpole!" cried the mayor.

"We'll get to that later. First I've got to find out what that beguiling scent is."

This time the President didn't wait for any more ideas from me. He took off running down the street. The Firemen's Band must have grown tired of "Hail to the Chief" because they switched to "Camp Town Races." The President picked up speed as he followed his nose this way and that. The whole crowd trotted along right behind him.

The President made a quick turn off Main Street onto Oak Street. Two blocks on Oak led to a left turn onto Maple Street. One block on Maple led to a right onto Acacia Avenue.

"Acacia Avenue! That's our street! Pop, the President is running down our street!" I said as we jogged along.

The President skidded to a halt directly in front of our house. The crowd froze. The band stopped playing. We watched as he lifted his nose, closed his eyes, and slowly turned around. When he opened his eyes, he was looking toward our backyard.

William Howard Taft, the twenty-seventh president of the United States, walked toward the back of our house. Then he saw it. Right there on the kitchen windowsill, freshly baked, sat Mom's apple pie.

As he picked up the pie, the President smiled. He held it high in one hand. He twirled in a circle like a ballerina. That's when Mom saw him.

She screamed and fell backward into the clothesline. Clothespins popped off in every direction, and socks, sheets, and shirts tumbled onto the lawn. The startled President lost his grip on the pie, and it went sailing through the air.

I leaped as high as I could and caught the pie in midair. Everyone cheered, and the band struck up a new tune—this time "For He's a Jolly Good Fellow."

Mom was so surprised that she couldn't speak. She just sat there, tangled in the clothesline, looking from the President to the yard full of people and back again.

The President apologized for causing such a commotion and helped her to her feet. "Ma'am," he asked politely, "was it you who baked that lovely pie?"

It didn't take Mom too long to invite the President in for some pie, and it didn't take him any time at all to accept. When he had finished his pie, Mom cut him another slice.

"Oh no, I couldn't," the President said, patting his stomach. He undid a vest button. "Well...maybe just one more."